Best Friend in the Whole World

Sandra Salsbury

Ω

PEACHTREE

ATLANTA

Roland lived deep in the woods all by himself.

He had a quiet life of drawing,

and music,

and drinking tea.

But sometimes he was lonely.

Often he would take walks in the woods,

wandering among the trees,

hoping,

just maybe,

to find...

...a friend!

"Hello," said Roland. "Are you also looking for a friend?"

Roland called his new friend Milton. They were perfect for each other.

Milton also loved drawing,

and music,

and drinking tea.

Together, they were happy.

One day, while on a walk in the woods,

Roland and Milton spotted something new.

"That kind of looks like you," said Roland.

"But your name is Milton."

"That can't be you," said Roland. "I found you on the path among the trees."

"Well, that's definitely not you," said Roland,

"because you love drawing, music, and tea."

"That's why you're my best friend
in the whole world."

"What's this?"

Back at home,

Roland could not forget
about the signs.

Soon, the lonely feelings from before all came tumbling back.

And everything was worse than ever.

Roland wondered if anyone else in the whole world was also feeling lonely.

So Roland paid a visit to the log by the lake.

"Hello?" said a voice, as the door opened.

"Oh, you found Popkin! I have been so worried!"

"Thank you," she said, "for bringing my best friend home."

Roland returned to his home all by himself.

Dear ~~Milton,~~ Popkin,
Thank you for spending a few days with me. I had a lot of fun and will miss you.

Your friend,
Roland

Without a best friend, life would be quiet again.

That night, Roland felt more lonely than ever.

So the next day, after some drawing, music, and tea,

Roland went for a walk in the woods.

As he wandered among
the trees, Roland realized…

...he knew exactly where to find a friend!

For Jacob, my best friend in the whole world
—S. S.

Published by
PEACHTREE PUBLISHING COMPANY INC.
1700 Chattahoochee Avenue
Atlanta, Georgia 30318-2112
www.peachtree-online.com

Edited by Kathy Landwehr
Composition by Adela Pons

The illustrations were rendered in watercolor.

Printed in October 2020 by Toppan Leefung Pte. Ltd
in China
10 9 8 7 6 5 4 3 2 1
First Edition
ISBN 978-1-68263-250-5

Cataloging-in-Publication Data is available from the
Library of Congress.